I0610055

Alfred Edward Pease

**The Badger**

A Monograph

Alfred Edward Pease

**The Badger**
*A Monograph*

ISBN/EAN: 9783337398842

Printed in Europe, USA, Canada, Australia, Japan

Cover: Foto ©Andreas Hilbeck / pixelio.de

More available books at **www.hansebooks.com**

# THE BADGER

## *A MONOGRAPH*

BY

## ALFRED E. PEASE, M.P.

AUTHOR OF
"THE CLEVELAND HOUNDS AS A TRENCHER-FED PACK,"
"HORSE BREEDING FOR FARMERS," ETC.

LONDON

LAWRENCE AND BULLEN, Ltd.
16, HENRIETTA STREET, COVENT GARDEN, W.C.
1898

" Hunting it is the noblest exercise,
  Makes men laborious, active, wise ;
  Brings health and doth the spirits delight ;
  It helps the hearing and the sight :
  It teacheth arts that never slip
  The memory—good horsemanship,
  Search, sharpness, courage, and defence,
  And chaseth all ill-habits thence."—BEN JONSON.

# THE BADGER

## PART I

I DO not know of the existence of any monograph on the Badger, ancient or modern, in English or any other language. Nor have I been able to find any adequate description in any work on natural history or British fauna of this the largest, and by no means the least interesting, of the real wild animals that still exist in England and Wales. So that, however unfitted I may be to write a scientific treatise on the last of the bear tribe that we have yet with us, I have ventured to think that my own observations and researches, with experiences of the chase of this troglodyte, may be of interest to lovers

B

of the animal world, and to not a few sportsmen.

From my boyhood all wild animals have had for me an intense fascination, and though in later years my hunting-grounds have been for the most part in other countries and continents, and among larger game, I doubt if any of the beasts whose acquaintance I have thus made has been a source of greater interest to me than the badger. The charm of an animal for man, where the sporting is the master instinct, appears to be measured by his capacity to elude observation and defy pursuit; and the badger, judged by this test, is a charming creature. I may be mistaken, but to me it appears that the chase in its widest sense is one of the best schools for studying nature. Such knowledge as I have gained of the badger has been due to the indulgence of this "brutal" instinct, as it is profanely called, and from quiet observation. If the reader will spare a little time, I will show him the manner in which my observations are made, but I warn him that there is nothing scientific about them. I have no microscope and no dissecting-room.

It is June. A hot summer's day is dying, and the sun is sinking through soft clouds of glory behind the pine woods on the hill. A thousand birds in vale and woodland are singing with an ecstasy and sweetness that seem tenderly conscious that the hours of song are numbered — that the days are coming when darkness or dawn will steal over the land in silence, unheralded as it is to-day by their wild sweet notes. We wander across the pasture by the cattle, and along the side of the ripening meadow towards the wooded bank under the edge of the moor, where the badger has his home. As we near the covert, a few rabbits that have ventured far out into the field frisk up the hill, alarming their less adventurous companions, and all make for the shelter of the wood, displaying a hundred little cotton tails.

As the gate into the plantation opens a few wood-pigeons stop their cooing and fly swiftly up and out of the trees with a clean cutting slap-slap of their wings to some other solitude safer from intrusion. Once in the shadow of the firs, softly treading we come up-wind to the badger " set." Here we choose a place among the larch stems which gives us a good view of the most-used entrances to the earth, some fifteen yards from the nearest hole. We turn up our coat-collars, draw our caps over our faces, and settle ourselves in such positions as will least try our patience and muscles during the hour in which we must remain immovable. In idea nothing could be more delightful than to sit in the deepening twilight of a summer's evening, with a soft breath of air stirring the feathery larch tops against the sky above, the ground carpeted with the vivid green of the opening bracken, surrounded by the music of cooing wood-pigeons, the full notes of blackbird and thrush, and listening to the pleasant sounds carried on the breeze from the distant farms.

Delightful as is the enjoyment of the con-fidences of Nature in her most hidden soli-tudes, the pleasure has its price, and the angler on a summer's eve can sympathize

with the man who sits over a badger earth.
But he at least can protect himself to some
extent against the exasperating attacks of
midges in myriads, and vent his feelings
aloud, and flog the waters, whilst the latter
must stoically endure the torture and the
plague. The most he can do is occasionally
to draw his hand from his pocket, and slowly
move it to his face and massacre the settlers
on his nose, his ears, his neck, and carefully
move it again into its hiding-place. In spite
of the torment, however, he may enjoy the
sights and sounds, known to but few, that
these witching hours alone can give. The
rabbits emerge within a yard of him, first the
little ones, unconscious of his eye, then the
old ones sit up and, imitating his immov-
ability, watch him critically with their black
beady eyes set, and noses palpitating; after
a while old paterfamilias gives his signal of
alarm or warning by a sharp pat, pat with
his hind foot, telling all round that there is
something in his vicinity he does not know
how to account for. The cry of the startled
blackbird warns that some other enemy is

on foot as he flies from the bur-tree to the thorn, and we see an old fox moving through the young bracken with lowered head and brush, starting off on his nightly raid. A belated squirrel throws himself from the tree above, runs close by us on the ground, up the stem of a larch, and is soon lost in the sea of green above. A numerous and dissipated family of little crested wrens, which should have settled for the night ere this, twitter with diminutive voices as they twist in and out and hang on the boughs of the spruce in front of us.

Gradually, as the daylight fades, one after another of the singers becomes silent, the sounds of day are hushed, and a perfect silence reigns in the twilight amidst the trees. Without any warning we are conscious of the clean black-and-white face of an old badger over the earthwork outside his hole, and presently he is all in view, sitting with bowed fore-legs and his head turning on his lithe outstretched neck, scenting the night air. There is nothing to excite his suspicion, so he shambles to the nearest

tree, puts up his fore-feet and rubs his neck,
smells round the well-known trunk, and
having satisfied himself that all is as usual,
sits for awhile admiring the limited landscape
before him. He then shuffles a few yards
from the earth, scratches the soil here and
there as if to keep his digging tools in order,
and returns to the bottom of the tree.
Another pied face appears, and more quickly
than the first she trundles off to join her
mate, and they bounce along one after another
over the earths, round the trees, down one
hole and out at another, and then rest awhile
outside the earth they first emerged from.
Three more come forth, and go through very
much the same programme as the first, snort-
ing and bumping along one after the other
and one against the other.

Presently one takes off into the thickest
covert. You can hear him bumping along,
sweeping through the bracken and crackling
the dead wood. Presently the others come
past you, tumbling along so close that you
could hit them with your stick. Probably
they take no notice, but if you wink, wince,

or move they will shamble back to the earth and watch you for ten minutes. It is then a trial for your nerves. If you move you have seen the last of them for the night, but if you succeed in being perfectly still they will recover sufficient confidence to sally forth again, but will take off quickly in different directions for their night's ramble. Then at last we may raise our stiff limbs and turn our steps through the dark woods, leaving the fox and badger to their devices, and once more frightening the rabbits which flash past us as we wade homewards through the grass heavy and wet with dew. We have made no startling discovery on this our first night together by the badger "set," but probably we have made a better acquaintance with badgers in this hour than we could have gained in any museum of natural history, with the assistance of the most erudite Fellow of the Zoological Society.

To understand and appreciate all sides of the badger's character you must see him in war as well as at peace ; and such knowledge has to be purchased by great labour and bodily fatigue. In the name of sport, as in the name of liberty, great crimes are often committed. There are those who look upon hunting of all sorts as cruel and degrading, and cannot understand the pleasures of a chase involving the distress of pursuit or pain to any animal. I have a certain sympathy for such sentiments, and yet, paradoxical as it may appear, my very love of animals increases my passion for hunting them. Besides the longing to come to close quarters with them, the desire to possess or to handle them, there is the natural ambition to be even with them. There is an unwritten code of honour in the field which, if followed, makes the struggle of wits and strength, of skill and endurance, a fair one, and one in which alone many a valuable lesson out of Nature's book can be taught. To relieve any tender consciences amongst my readers I may here declare, without wishing to reflect on brother sportsmen whose methods are more Cromwellian, that when victorious in the war with a badger, when, after many a hard-fought battle in his sub-

terranean fortress—when mine and counter-
mine, tunnel, shaft, and trench have driven
him fighting to his last stand in his deepest
and innermost citadel, and he has been
forced to capitulate—I have never abandoned
him to a victorious soldiery howling for
blood, but have always given him honourable
terms. I have never willingly or wantonly
killed a badger; he has invariably become
a pampered prisoner, or been transported to
some new home, where some one whom I
had interested in his species was prepared to
give him protection, and a new start in life.
Among those who have given my badgers
protection I may name Mr. Edward North
Buxton, who has done so much to maintain
the natural beauty of Epping Forest, and to
protect wild life within its borders. I know
of several thriving colonies of badgers within
the forest precincts descended from my
prisoners of war.

I have kept many badgers in confinement,
but never to "try" my dogs, and all my
terriers learnt their trade in legitimate
fashion. Badger-baiting I unreservedly con-

demn—it is as much a profanation of sport as coursing bagged hares in enclosed grounds. There are degrees of wickedness, and when a badger is placed in a properly-constructed badger-box there are few terriers that would not be vanquished in the encounter. The figure below illustrates the correct box.

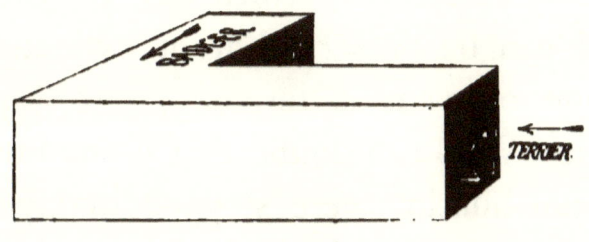

FIG. 1.

One of the atrocious methods by which the badger was baited in the last century is described and denounced in volume xii. of the *Sporting Magazine*, 1788. "They dig a place in the earth about a yard long, so that one end is four feet deep. At this end a strong stake is driven down. Then the badger's tail is split, a chain put through it, and fastened to the stake with such ability that the badger can come up to the other

end of the place. The dogs are brought
and set upon the poor animal, who sometimes destroys several dogs before it is
killed."

Badger-baiting, it seems, was the price the
race had to pay for its existence, and with
the happy disuse of a brutal sport the harmless badger has been doomed to extinction.
The only method by which any British wild
animal can be preserved from extinction in
this age of what is termed progress, is to
hunt it. Who can doubt, that if fox-hunting
and otter-hunting were stopped to-day, both
these creatures would be extinct within the
next few years? It may be a hard bargain
to make with them, but considering their
own crimes of violence, and their incompati-
bility with "civilization," it does not seem to
be a too severe condition to impose on the
fox and the otter, that if they are permitted
to live they must at least submit to the risks
and fortunes of the chase. Not being able
to do more than speculate on the intellectual
and nervous capacity of animals, we are apt
to assign to them some measure of human

powers of thought and feeling. Undoubtedly
they are physically less sensitive, and we
probably err when we ascribe to them more
than a slight ability to anticipate, or credit
them with such sentiments as anxiety, mental
distress, and those thoughts and sensations
that in the main make pain intolerable.
Those species that have long been associated
with man have, I think, a greater capacity
for suffering. The individuality of each
domestic race has been developed; the
difference of temperament and character of
each individual becomes more marked, and
more or less humanized, according to the
influences by which it is surrounded. There
is a more uniform character and greater similarity of temperament among wild animals,
and the more refined the civilization and the
more cultivated the senses, the more sensitive will the whole animal become. This
may be seen in the most common of Nature's
operations. The wild beast produces its
young with ease and without pain. With
woman, raised amidst the refinements of
civilization, the same operation is with every

precaution and assistance sometimes a danger-
ous, always an agonizing ordeal.

No, the terms are not hard. Take the
case of a fox, the most hunted of animals.
The ordinary lot of a fox compared with that
of any other creature, wild or domestic, or
even with man himself, is not an unenviable
one. Unlike the domestic animals, he is not
born into servitude or to die in early life by
the butcher's knife or axe. Happier than
man, he lives his life, whether longer or
shorter, free from the worries, cares, and the
thousand ills which flesh is heir to. The
fox's life is free as air. Protected for the
most part from the natural consequences
of his marauding disposition, fair play is
given to him to avoid the punishment he
deserves by the exercise of that strategy,
activity, and endurance with which he is
so abundantly endowed. Two or three
days in the three hundred and sixty-five
he may have to exert himself more or less
to save his brush, or the end may come
swiftly and suddenly after a long run; but
even so, are there not many of us who would

be glad to know that our death would come as swiftly and painlessly to us as to the fox, who, flying for forty minutes before the pack, confident, perhaps, to the last that he is a match for his pursuers, is rolled over in his stride? The sportsman may pity the sinking fox, with every desire to see the victory of the straining pack, in the moment when, after gallantly standing up before hounds, a straight-necked veteran finds he has shot his last bolt, and turns with fire yet in his eye to meet death in its swiftest form.

There is something strange in the mixture of pain with pleasure. My little son comes out cub-hunting with me in the early morning of a September day. He is the picture of delight, sitting on his pony among the hounds, the effigy of enjoyment as he follows them with his and his pony's head just above the high bracken, the incarnation of satisfaction as he receives his first brush and is blooded. He is none the less a little sportsman for sobbing himself to sleep at night with his brush hugged under the bedclothes, because of the thought that the bright little cubs he saw killed will never again run in and out of the wood on the hillside as of yore. I look into his room the following day, and find him in his night-shirt busy extracting the tail-bone from his trophy, and he stops in his work only to ask when the hounds will be out again.

The power of enjoying hunting of any sort is no evidence of want of tenderer feelings. It may be that the days of sport are numbered by the exigencies of what is termed the progress of civilization; but whether men's hearts will be braver, their bodies and minds healthier, or their natures kindlier and happier for the change, only time may show. All this is something in the nature of apology; but, excuse or none, thousands are conscious that the nearest approach to pure unmixed pleasure that they have known has been derived from the chase, where cares are forgotten, pulses quickened, eyes brightened, and the mind refreshed. About conscious or unconscious vicarious sacrifice with regard to the badger I will not say more than this, that the baiting of an animal in confinement, even though he be but the scapegoat for a thousand of his kind, is so repugnant to humanity, and so likely to breed cruelty, that though I lament his imminent extinction I would say, "perish *Meles taxus*" rather than let him pay this price for the continuance of his race, and, whatever view he might have himself, I would refuse him the option.

The badger has made a wonderful struggle for existence, and may linger on for many years yet in the more secluded corners of England and Wales (in Scotland he is almost extinct), but he owes all to his own mysterious silent ways, and nothing to man's mercy in the matter. The intelligent and unprejudiced wearers of velveteen, who, with the tacit consent of their masters, have by means of the steel trap, flag-trap, and gun, exterminated and banished for ever the most interesting of our animals and the most beautiful of our birds, have hitherto failed in their ruthless attempt to rid earth and heaven of everything but furred and feathered game, so far as the badger is concerned. In many

English counties, however, the badger has given in before ceaseless digging, snaring, and shooting, and the silent covert where he had his earth, where he dug and delved and made his wonderful subterranean stronghold, knows him no more. He has gone with the polecat, the pine marten, the wild cat, the harriers, the buzzards, and a host of the brightest and loveliest of our birds. Guiltless of the crimes of his fellow-victims against game, he was and is still ignorantly classed under that all-embracing word of the keeper, "vermin." There are few who lament his disappearance save perhaps the makers of shaving-brushes, and the old people whose faith in the efficacy of "badger-grease" can no longer find the opportunity of exercising the same. This faith is an old one. I read in the *Sporting Magazine*, 1800, volume xvii. —"The flesh, blood, and grease of the badger are very useful for oils, ointments, salves, and powders, for shortness of breath, the cough of the lungs, for the stone, sprained sinews, coll-achs, etc. The skin, being well dressed, is very warm and comfortable for ancient people who are troubled with paralytic disorders." Evidently a few badgers in the good old days supplied the place of the country doctor. About the fancied or really mischievous habits of the badger I shall have something to say later on.

# PART II

THE badger (*Meles taxus*, or *Ursus meles*) is known under various aliases, viz. the Brock (Danish *Broc*, Erse *Broc*, Welsh *Brock*), the Pate, and the Grey. Of these the Brock is perhaps the commonest, and is the name most used in the north of England. There is an expression common in the north that would lead the ignorant to believe that a badger perspires, or sweats, viz. " sweating like a brock." In Yorkshire I often hear a man say, " Ah. sweats like a brock," and the user of this elegant metaphor innocently imagines he is perspiring like a badger. But "brock " is the old north-country word for the insect known as " cuckoo-spit " (*Aphrophora spumaria*), which covers itself in the larval state with froth and foam (cf. Welsh *broch*, foam)—*vide* Atkinson's *Dictionary of the Cleveland Dialect.* In parts of Cornwall and Wales the word " Grey " may be in use, but I myself have only come across it in books, more especially old ones. Though able to boast these several titles, there is but one species known in Europe, and in general appearance he is the same animal, though varying locally in size and shade of colour. He has been classed as belonging to the bear tribe, but the badger is really a single species and a sub-genus in itself. The dentition of a badger is half tuberculous and half carnivorous, and in this respect approaches the martens.

About few animals has there been more nonsense written in regard to habits and anatomy, and for many of the popular notions concerning the badger there is no foundation whatever. In the ancient books descriptive of sport and wild animals we read that there were in England two kinds of badger—the one as we know it, and the other a " pig-badger," with cloven hoofs and other attributes of the porker. It is astonishing how these old authors drew upon their imagination, and where they found suggestions for their errors. In this case it may be they were misled by the custom, which still continues, of distinguishing between the dog and bitch, or male and female badger, by using the terms boar and sow ; or it may be the idea dawned whilst they ate their rasher from a badger ham !

There are altogether not more than five (or perhaps six) kinds of badger known throughout the world, so far as I know.[1]

1. The European badger, known over almost the whole of Europe and Asia. 2. A larger species, confined to the high steppes of Eastern Siberia. 3. The North American mistonusk, or chocaratouch (*Meles labradorica* or *hudsonius*). 4. The Mexican badger, found south of latitude 35 degrees. 5. The Japanese badger. 6. The Indian badger

---

[1] Lydekker, whose authority I accept, enumerates four kinds of badger—
1. The American (*Taxidea americana*).
2. The Common (*Meles taxus*).
3. Malayan (*Mydaus meliceps*).
4. The Sand-badger (*Arctonyx collaris*).

(*Meles indica*) might be added perhaps, though it has a pig's snout, long legs, and long tail. Its native name is bhalloo-soor, *i. e.* the bear pig.

Nos. 3 and 4, the chocaratouch and Mexican, differ so distinctly from the others in dentition, though in appearance similar to the European species, that a new genus, Taxidea, has been established for their reception.[1]

Popular error, and old writers, describe the badger as having his legs shorter on one side than the other, and the latter, with philosophical ingenuity, have discovered therein a wonderful provision of nature; for, says Nicholas Cox, " He hath very sharp Teeth, and therefore is accounted a deep-biting beast; his back is broad, and his legs are longer on the right side than the left, and therefore he runneth best when he gets on the side of an Hill or a Cart roadway." The same author also states—" Her manner

---

[1] In Lower California there is a variety of badger which differs from described forms by its dark colouration and broad nuchal stripe.

is to fight on her back, using thereby both her Teeth and her Nails, and by blowing up her Skin after a strange and wonderful manner she defendeth herself against any blow and teeth of Dogs. Only a small stroke on her Nose will dispatch her presently. You may thrash your heart weary on her back, which she values as a matter of nothing." If such a provision in the matter of legs did exist, one can realize the comfort of the uneven legs on a hill-side, but what gravels us is the discomfort of the return journey! The rolling, shambling gait that characterizes the badger is doubtless the origin of this absurd theory, which might be equally applied to any other member of the bear family. The European badger, as we find him in England, Wales, Scotland, and Ireland, stands about ten to twelve inches from the ground, has a long, stout body, with the belly near the earth. He has a coat so long and dense, and legs so short, that he appears to travel very nearly *ventre à terre*. The male is somewhat larger than the female, and weighs more. The weight of a male is about 25 lbs., that of a female about 22 lbs. When they are fat, or in grease in September, they will scale more. Badgers have been known to weigh up to about 40 lbs.; the largest I ever dug out and weighed was an old lean dog badger that scaled over 35 lbs.

The head of the badger is wedge-shaped in general conformation, the back of the head large, the cheek-bones well sprung, and the muzzle fine and long. The nose or snout is black in colour, long and full; the eyes small, black, or black-blue; and the ears small, round, close-set, and neat. The strength of a badger's legs is most remarkable, and for his size (the animal only weighs from 19 lbs. to 35 lbs.) he possesses a most wonderful combination of bone and muscle. The legs are very short and the joints large; the feet, like the legs, are nearly black, and are large and long. The badger is a plantigrade, that is, when travelling he puts down the whole of his foot, including the heel, flat on the ground. His fore-feet are larger, longer, and better equipped for digging than his hind, but all are armed with long, sharp claws, and it is prodigious what he can effect with them. There is no mistaking his tracks —no animal's footprint is in the least like his. His heel is large and wide; this, and his four round, plump toes, leave an impression in sand, mud, or snow that cannot be confounded with any other. If the mud is deep, or there is snow on the ground, he also leaves the mark of his claws, but as a rule these are not observable, as he puts his weight on the sole of his foot—his tracks are usually almost in a line. The badger is cut out for a miner. His wedge-shaped head is capable of forcing a passage through sand and soft strata, whilst his armour-tipped diggers are worked by machinery that rivals in power the steam navvy; and whilst his fore-feet are going like an engine, throwing stones, bits of rock, sand, clay, and all that he comes in contact with between his fore-legs (which are set wide apart, leaving plenty of room under the chest), his powerful hams are working his hind-legs and feet like little demons, throwing back all that the fore-feet throw under his belly. And this is not all. His powerful jaw and teeth will cut, break, and tear all roots that obstruct his passage onwards, and it is most entertaining to see him going through earth, shale, and stone with the rapidity and sustained energy of a machine. No one who has not seen it would credit what one of these animals can do. I have often been defeated by their being able to penetrate more quickly than even a gang of men with pick-axe, spade, shovels, and crow-bar could follow. And it is safe to say that as long as a terrier is not up to the badger, the badger is not only advancing quicker than the men (if his earth is on a hill-side), but has also, in nine cases out of ten, barri-caded his retreat and scored a victory. I have known a badger, left for awhile by the terrier, bore his way straight up out to day-light and escape. The badger is covered with a thick, long-haired coat, which with a loose skin of extraordinary density and tough-ness forms a complete and effective armour. The hair on his head is short and smooth, and the sharp, clean black-and-white markings of his head give a very pretty and effective appearance to it. The general appearance in colour of a badger is a sort of silvery-grey, turning to black on the throat, breast, belly, and legs. Inverting the usual colouring of other animals, which is generally dark on the back, with lighter colouring on the belly and under the arms and thighs, the badger is lighter on the back and black underneath.

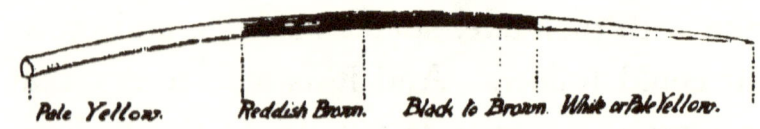

Pale Yellow.    Reddish Brown.    Black to Brown. White or Pale Yellow.

FIG. 2.

Not only is this colouring peculiar to the badger, but his hair is unlike that of any other creature known to me, being light at the root and darker above.

The colour of a badger alters with age. The little cubs, till they are seven or eight months old, are a clean, bright, light silvery-grey ; they then become yellower in their coats, a colour which they keep sometimes permanently, but which they generally change after two years for a suit of darker, purer grey. The badger's tail is about five inches long, covered with long, coarse, lighter-coloured hair than that on his body, and is of a yellowish-brown colour.

The badger has another peculiar distinction that is somewhat mysterious, viz. a pouch, the vent of which is close under the root of the tail, and contains an oily fœtid matter which he has the power of emitting. Different uses have been ascribed to this provision, such as that which ferrets and polecats have. I have never noticed a badger use it as has been suggested, as a mode of defence or annoyance, and am sure that this is not its purpose. But there is no doubt the badger sucks and licks this substance, whether by way of taking a tonic, a cooling draught, a stimulant, or other physic I cannot say. I am, however, inclined to believe that from this source he is able to maintain his health and support life during those periods of seclusion and total retirement in his " earth " which have led naturalists to describe him as a hibernating animal.

In this theory I am strengthened by a
French author, Edmond Le Masson, who
writes—" The badger does not always give
evidence of his presence in his woody retreat.
. . . There, should one go to see him, he
may, from pure idleness, remain shut up, it
being easy for him to support himself during
the longest period of retirement by licking
the secretion which oozes from the pouch
under his tail." The author goes on to give
an account which was sent to the French
papers by M. Récopé, Garde Général at
Marly-le-Roi, of a badger that was shut in a
culvert without any food whatever for forty-
five days, walled in on every side, and where
no tree root could penetrate. A gamekeeper,
a noted trapper, had blocked the exit, and
tried in every way he could devise to trap
him, from February 18, 1853, to April 4,
and when at last he succumbed to a ruse of
the keeper's he was quite lively, and weighed
nearly 19 lbs. It appears that however carefully his traps were set in the mouth of the
exit, the badger came every night and rolled
on them and struck them, as they will do

when they suspect any human infernal machine. That he will remain for a week or two at a time without issuing from his "earth" is certain, but the most casual observer will see badger tracks in the snow in the severest weather, and I have never been able to find that there were no tracks in the snow issuing from the "earths" in winter for more than a week or two at a time. The badger is less active, eats less, goes fewer and shorter journeys in winter, and has a hibernating tendency; but the idea that the British species shuts himself up and takes to his bed through the winter months, and never comes forth till spring, is a fallacy.

Having attempted a slight description of the badger as far as his exterior is concerned, I shall leave to "Dryasdust" the description and nomenclature of the badger's interior economy, as well as the enumeration, weights, and measurements of his bones and muscles. He possesses, however, one or two structural peculiarities that deserve a little attention. There is much similarity in the general conformation of the badger's and bear's skull, but the protecting ridge on the head is absent in the bear. What gives to the badger's jaw its proverbial and terrific force? To witness its work is to know that its power of biting, crushing, and holding must be the result of some peculiarly strong mechanical as well as muscular construction. The examination of the skull helps in the solution of the mystery.

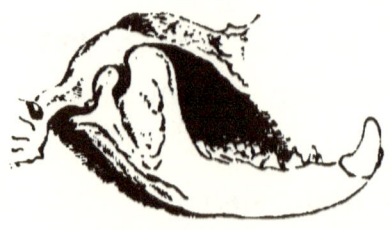

FIG. 3. Lower Jaw of Badger.

The conformation of the jaw is strong, and the muscles attached to it powerful; but besides this he has two distinguishing structural additions that give his jaws, furnished with his formidable teeth, the strength and retentive power of an iron vice. The first is that his lower jaws are locked into sockets in the skull, and are thereby made—unlike those of all other animals I know of—

impossible of dislocation.[1]   His head or skull, when stripped of flesh and bare, still retains the lower jaws in such a way that they cannot be displaced without fracturing the massive bones of the head or jaw. The teeth of a badger require respectful attention. There are eighteen teeth in the lower and sixteen in the upper jaw, in all thirty-four. The four big molars, two above and two

FIG. 4. Dovetailed Jaws.

below, are large and strong, the upper being much the larger and wider ones, the lower being longer and fitting within the upper, as do all the lower teeth. The four canines are large, thick, round, long and formidable, and are his chief weapons. The lower canines dovetail when the jaws close with the upper,

[1] The curved ridges of bone on the skull by which the lower jaw is held in its place by gripping the condyle are more or less well developed in most of the weasel family.

but all the four points or ends turn outward and backward.

The second peculiarity arises from a high ridge of bone, standing straight up and running from the base of the skull to between the ears, giving a firm hold to the ligaments

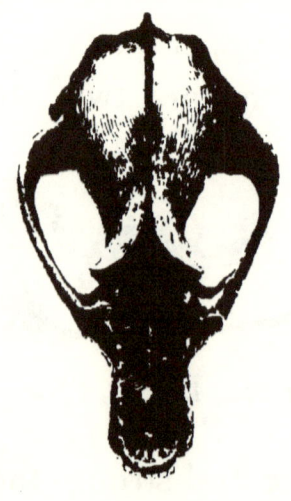

Fig. 5. Skull of Badger—front view.

and tendons, and an additional leverage and length, which are again rendered more effective by passing over the high cheekbones as over a pulley before reaching the jaws. There is a saying that "a badger never leaves go till he makes his teeth meet," and there is a foundation of truth in

34

it. The length of time he will hold on to the limb of an enemy is certainly fearful, and the way in which his thick strong canines go through the bone. On one occasion, in Wales, a keeper residing near the place I was staying at thought he saw the badger's tail at the end of a badger-digging, and laid

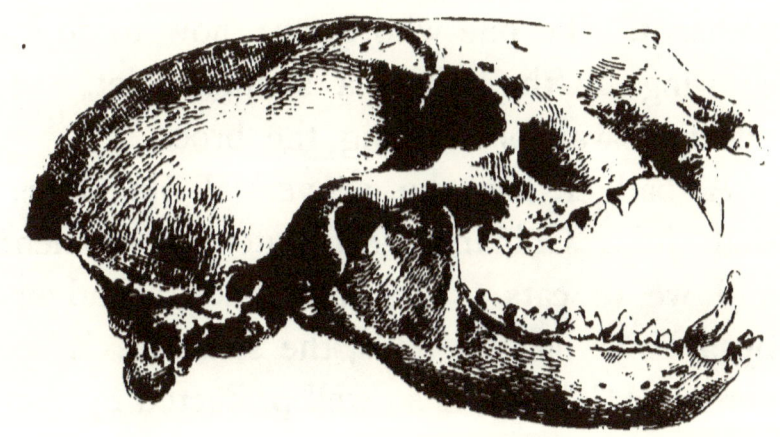

Fig. 6. Skull—side view.

hold of it to draw him. He had made a terrible mistake, and had got hold of a hind-foot. The badger held him by the wrist for ten minutes with his arm stretched up the hole; when he let go his hold the hand was hanging by a few shreds, and had, of course, to be amputated. I have always drawn a badger when possible by the tail, as the use of the tongs is sometimes difficult, especially in certain holes and at great depths, and there is a liability for the tongs to give way, and then the badger charges in your face or through your legs. I have seen a badger's teeth break and fly off in chips from iron tongs, a sight and sound that is not pleasant. To one who knows how to do it, drawing by the tail is a simple, quiet, and effective way of "taking the brock."

A badger has the proverbial nine lives that John Chinaman attributes to women and we to cats. You cannot kill a badger by a blow on the head, the structure is so dense. His brain is so well protected by the ridges of bone along his skull and over his eye-sockets, and by the strength and pro-jection of his cheek-bones, as to make him all but invulnerable in that quarter. His skin is so thick and tough, and his coat so heavy and coarse, that shot will scarcely penetrate it ; but he has one place as tender as a nigger's shins, and that is his nose, where, if he is struck once, he is instantly dispatched. I was witness of a scene in the hunting field with the Cleveland hounds during the mastership of the late Mr. Henry Turner Newcomen, which, however disgusting, illustrated the vitality of the badger. We thought we had run a fox to ground in a drain. The terriers were sent for, one was put in to bolt him, but after a quarter of an hour's attempt he came out, having given it up, with severe marks of punishment. One that could be depended on was then dispatched to ground, and digging operations commenced. As time went on we thought from the sound that it could not be a fox, and presently there was a charge down the drain, and a badger came bouncing and floundering out among the crowd of bystanders, the terrier holding on to him. The other terriers, barking furiously to join in the fray, excited the hounds in an adjoining field ; they broke out past the whips, and nineteen couple were soon at the badger, who was entirely lost to view in the struggling and worrying mass. But he was plying his jaws all the time, as was evidenced by the howls of pain from the wounded hounds as they withdrew from this unaccustomed entertainment. The whips and others did their best to flog the hounds off, but this was not accomplished for at least ten minutes. After much bloodshed, and when the last hound had been choked off, the badger showed neither scratch nor wound, and looked as fresh as possible. Mr. Newcomen ordered a whip to despatch him and end the tragedy. The whip clubbed a weighted hunting-stock, striking him several smashing blows on the head, and left him apparently dead. A farmer having asked if he might have him to stuff, put him in a sack and carried him off. A few days later I met the farmer, Mr. R. Brunton, of Marton, and he told me that when he got home the badger was as lively as ever, so he put him on a collar and chain and fastened him to a kennel. The day following he thought, from the appearance of the badger, that he was hurt about the head, and with some difficulty examined him, and found that the lower jaw was injured. He thereupon got a revolver and fired a shot into his ear, and then he assured me the badger only shook his head. He was so taken aback that for a moment or two he thought of giving up the attempt to kill him, but firing a second ball into him behind the shoulder he put an end at once to the poor brute's sufferings.

The badger, as I have said, is becoming very scarce in England, and is decreasing in numbers in France and other countries as well. There are, however, several English and Welsh counties where in woodlands he still is to be found in considerable numbers, and some districts where they are common enough. The badger is fairly plentiful in many parts of Cornwall, Devon, Dorset, Somerset, Hants, and Gloucestershire, along the Welsh border, and in Mid and South Wales. It is to be found also in Sussex, Wilts, occasionally in Surrey and Kent, and here and there through the Midland and home counties. It is becoming rare in the north of England, but still lingers in the North Riding of Yorkshire, chiefly in the districts of the hills and moors between

Scarborough and York. In Lincolnshire it is to be found in places; it is extinct in Durham, and practically so in Northumberland, where within fifty years it was common enough.

A Northumberland gamekeeper of my father's has told me he knew it in the Kyloe Craggs and the Howick Woods, and remembered his father taking him to see their dog tried at a badger near Belford. In none of these places are they to be found now. In my own district of Cleveland they were in 1874 all but extinct. I remember as a boy two were caught in our neighbourhood, one in Kildale and one at Ayton; but in 1874 I had three young badgers sent me from Cornwall, dug out by one of my uncles, and these I turned out in my father's coverts, and secured for them the keeper's protection. Since then they have, with a few later introductions, held their own, and a few years ago I knew of nine badger " sets " in the vicinity, and some five on our own ground; but I regret that the hands of neighbours are against them.

In Scotland the badger is now rare. In the north-eastern counties, where till recently he was to be met with in every wild woodland and forest district, he has entirely vanished. In Ross-shire and in the west he is occasionally found in places where the wild cat and marten are making their last stand against the keeper and his exterminating engine, the steel trap. In Ireland the badger is still found in the Wild West. I have come upon him in Connemara, near the Killery harbour, and have heard of him in Kerry and other counties.

As to the distribution of the badger in Ireland I quote the following interesting letters from the *Field*:—

"'Lepus Hibernicus' may be glad to know that the badger is still fairly common in the neighbourhood of Clonmel. The country people, who know them better under the name of 'earth-dogs,' in distinction to 'water-dogs,' or otters, not unfrequently catch them in one way or another, and offer them for sale. Fortunately for the badger the demand is extremely limited."—Badger (Clonmel).

" Permit me to coincide with 'Lepus Hibernicus' respecting the plentifulness of the
badger in Ireland. Some years since I was
on a large estate in Co. Clare, and badgers
were abundant on the domain and the adjoining property ; I also found them numerous
in the wilds of Galway. I have found and
killed them in many parts of England and
Wales, but have seen and trapped far more
in the west of Ireland."—J. J. M. "Your
correspondent, 'Lepus Hibernicus,' in the
*Field* of November 5, mentions that badgers
are by no means uncommon in Ireland. I
am in the west of Cornwall, and there are
any amount here, a great deal too plentiful
to please me, as I am sure they do a lot
of harm to rabbits and game. I found the
parts of a fowl in a field, evidently killed by
a badger, as there was a trail not a foot
away, and also a hole scratched, which could
be the work of none other than a badger. I
had two very big ones brought to me alive
last week. They were caught by setting a
noose of thin rope in their run. I should
like to know a good way to exterminate

them, as, though I shoot over a great deal of ground, I have never seen one out in daytime, but their trail is everywhere."—H. J. W. "The badger is by no means rare in the west of Clare, where I have trapped several."—A. H. G. "I beg to inform 'Lepus Hibernicus' that badgers are by no means scarce in this place."—A. R. Warren, Warren's Court, Lisarda, Cork. "The badger in this part of the Co. Cork is certainly not rare—Owen, Sheehy, Coosane, and Goulacullen mountains, with the adjoining ranges, afford shelter to a goodly number. Farm hands occasionally capture unwary ones, and offer them for sale as pets, or to test the mettle of the national terrier, or to be converted into bacon. A badger's ham is often seen suspended from the rafter of a farmer's kitchen."—J. Wagner (Dunmanway, Co. Cork).

The counties in which I have had most acquaintance with the badger have been Radnorshire, Yorkshire, Herefordshire, Gloucestershire, and Cornwall, but perhaps most of my experience has been gained in the last-named county, as far as digging for him is concerned; whilst it is at home in Cleveland that I have watched him for nearly twenty years, and gained some knowledge of his mode of life and habits. I am not sure whether there are not a few still left in the Cheviots and the districts of the Upper Tyne and Tweed. Up till about 1850 they were to be found on the Cleveland hills, or rather on their wooded sides and in the "gills." The last place where I heard of them being hunted was in the ravine and woods of Kilton.

A badger's earth or warren is properly and generally called a "set" or "cete." They vary in respect of size, number of entrances, depth of galleries, and choice of site almost as much as rabbit-holes. Sometimes badgers will find sufficient room in rocks to make a home, and it is extraordinary the excavations they occasionally make in apparently solid rock. Usually, however, they select some softer material in which to make their underground passages and chambers. They will choose a quiet hillside away from man's habitation, amongst the whin bushes, or in the woods near a stream or small runner of water. Such a "set," if long established, will penetrate through earth, clay, and sub-soil, to some stratum of shale, or sand, or loose rock. Some of the galleries and chambers will be at a great distance from the surface, and some at an enormous depth. When a new earth is made I have always found the badger appropriate the holes of rabbits, and proceed to excavate, enlarge, and open them out. This operation of open-ing a new earth takes place constantly in the spring-time, great masses of material be-ing thrown out; but as often as not the new house is abandoned before completed, and the subsequent labours of the family are devoted to repairing, enlarging, and making new front or back doors to the old place. In Cornwall I once tried my hand with my brother, some strong Cornishmen, and a team of terriers, at a very innocent-looking badger "set" situated in a level field. There were but three holes, and these not very far apart. The farmer told us that there had been badgers there all his life, and no one had ever been able to dig one out. This rather stimulated us than otherwise, and we had in the course of a few hours dug a trench some six feet deep, and were nearing the sounds of the subterranean conflict, which had been sustained by the terriers, when suddenly we found that we were above the sound, and we sank a shaft down three feet from the bottom of our trench, to find galleries and chambers in all directions. The battle had by this time moved, and we were in despair at the prospect of following on the level with a depth of nine feet of surface soil to be lifted in every direction we turned. I was listening at the bottom of the trench, having penetrated to the third storey of this underground barrack, when I distinctly heard the "bump-bump" of the badger below me. My companions came down and listened too, and there was not the slightest doubt that there was a fourth storey and labyrinth of passages some three or four feet below us, and for anything we knew another beyond. The day was far spent, the task was impossible, and the rest of our time was devoted to getting the terriers out, and making as good a retreat as we could before the victorious enemy.

I should think this "set" was hundreds of years old, and some of the passages, the farmer told us, were a hundred yards long! As a rule a badger's hole descends rapidly at first, and then may branch into any number of by-ways and subterranean galleries. Whichever route you follow, however, you invariably come to a chamber or "oven," which is generally a sort of vaulted hall, where four ways meet, and which is, or has been, the living-room of the family at some previous time. Where there is an old-established "set" it is difficult to drive the badgers permanently away from it. They may leave it for a while from fancy, or because of disturbance, but they will certainly return.

The badger and his wife have a regular spring cleaning after the winter is over, and about March and April a cart-load of winter bedding, rubbish, earth, and sweepings will be thrown in a few nights outside the front door. There is generally the old bedding left in one or two of the big chambers for the lady who is to be brought to bed in February, March, or April; and there is another turn-out after this interesting event has been accomplished. About the middle of June, in July and August, and as late as October and November, an extraordinary amount of fresh bedding will be taken in. On summer evenings I have watched the badgers at work, but regret that I cannot substantiate the following description:—

"Badgers when they Earth, after by digging they have entred a good depth, for the clearing of the Earth out, one of them falleth on the back, and the other layeth Earth on the belly, and so taking his hinder feet in the mouth draweth the Belly-laden Badger out of the Hole or Cave; and having disburdened herself, re-enters and doth the like till all be finished."

No, this is not how it is done, though it is a curious sight to see the real thing. The badger will come out, take a look round, and sit awhile close to the mouth of the hole.

He will then shuffle about and get further from the hole. You will watch him descend into some bracken-covered hollow, and will see nothing more of him for awhile. Then you will hear him gently pushing and shoving and grunting, and know that he is very busy over something. He will reappear bumping along backwards, a heap of bracken and of grass or old straw, left from a pheasant feed, under his belly, and encircled by his arms and fore-feet. He will continue this most undignified and curious mode of retrogression to the earth, and will disappear tail first down his hole, still hugging and tugging at his burden.

" It is very pleasant to behold them when they gather materials for their Couch, as straw, leaves, moss, and such-like; for with their Feet and their Head they will wrap as much together as a man will carry under his arm, and will make shift to get into their Cells and Couches " (*The Gentleman's Recreation*).

I have not seen a badger make more than two such excursions by daylight, but have no doubt that after dark a considerable number of such journeys ·may be accomplished. For weeks together, on any morning, you may see the litter of bracken and grass strewing the way to his home and down the various entrances.

And now let me again, with all possible respect, put some of our scientific friends right. It is not often that an amateur can ; but a man who is not able to tell you everything, as these learned men do, about every living creature, may from a country life and experience be able to correct some errors in respect of one animal at least. M. Buffon, the immortal and wonderful natural historian, tells us that the badger is a solitary animal. This is the reverse of truth ; he is less solitary than the fox. He is fond of company ; he is monogamous, and clings closely and faithfully to his own wife. With badgers, as with the human race, the sexes are not precisely equal in numbers, and often, from the force of circumstances, a badger has to remain a celibate, but he is not a bachelor by choice. He may become a widower, but in either case he will travel far to seek a partner to share his shelter and his lot. It is not altogether rare to find an old solitary dog badger, who has loved and lost, or taken in late age to a hermit's cell ; but he, as often as not, when he has failed to secure the companionship of the gentler sex, has found some other male to share his home, when they can live comfortably *en garçon.*

Nor do the married pair shun the society of their kind. I have often seen large badger "sets" almost as full of badgers as a warren is of rabbits. One evening, near my house, I waited an hour of midge-plagued time to watch the badgers come out from a small "set," and was rewarded by seeing a procession of seven full-grown badgers emerge from a single hole, and I had them all in full view for something like twenty minutes. As this was in July they could hardly be one family. They were every one more than a year old, and a badger's family is usually two in number, sometimes three, and never more than four ; and this last is exceedingly

rare in my experience. In no sense, therefore, is the badger solitary. Indeed I have
actually known myself several instances of
a badger and fox living in apparent amity
in the same earth, whilst I hardly ever saw a
badger "earth" that was not either itself or
the immediate vicinity tenanted by rabbits.
As to the consistency of any friendship that
exists between badgers and foxes and rabbits,
I shall have more to say later on. I have,
however, taken a badger and rabbit out of
the same hole lying side by side. The
badger is said to be the protector of the
rabbit. He does not altogether deserve
this title, and the rabbit enjoys the immunity
in a badger's earth chiefly from the fact that
the badger cannot follow it in the smaller
holes without digging, an effort which in
his estimation is, as a rule, not worth the
candle.

Buffon dwells on the cleanliness of the
badger. He certainly is not the stinking
animal he is accused of being. His house
and himself are as a rule bright and cleanly
looking, and it is only when in confinement,

and deprived of the sanitary arrangements
to which he is accustomed, that he becomes
offensive. Writers are not correct in saying
that he never deposits his dung in his earth,
but as a rule he does not, and his habit is
to go some little distance from his home, dig
a hole, and there leave his excrement. He
will use the same hole for a few days, and
then cover it up with earth and make a new
one. There is a smell about a badger
"earth," but it is not disagreeable, and nothing like so rank and strong as that of a
fox's. He is, however, often troubled with
lice and ticks, so that it is desirable when
your dogs have been to ground carefully to
wash them. But in this respect a badger is
not worse than sheep and goats, and with
such a coat as he has it is no wonder that
it is sometimes tenanted. The same distinguished authority states that the badger
produces its young in summer, but I have
never known this happen. March is the
usual month, and the rule is not earlier than
February nor later than April. A naturalist
at Cambridge told me that he knew of a

badger bitch that was many months in confinement (I think he said eighteen months),
and gave birth to cubs—but I was not convinced of the accuracy of his statement that
she had never had access to one of her kind.
It is only fair to mention that Vyner, in his
*Notitia Venatica*, states that "It is a fact
perhaps not generally known, nevertheless
curious, that badgers go twelve months with
young. This fact I *learned from a neighbour of mine in Warwickshire*, who some
years ago dug out in the spring a sow badger.
She was confined in an outhouse for twelve
months, at about which period she produced ·
one young one. During her confinement it
was impossible for her to have been visited
by a male."

That an animal of this size should go with
young for such a period is so extraordinary,
and so great an exception to the ordinary
provisions of nature, that the theory requires
much greater support than mere hearsay
evidence. If it were a fact, or if it were
the rule, the evidence to support the theory
of twelve months' gestation should be over-

whelming, considering the number of badgers
that are in confinement. I have had many
in confinement for long periods, and have
never known them to give any evidence in
support of this theory. I have kept a pair
for a long period, but, like many other wild
animals in confinement, they never bred.
All sorts of theories exist as to the period
of gestation in badgers, but I think I shall
be very near the mark when I say that they
go with young about nine weeks, and I con-
ceive that the mistake made by those who
have thought that they go over a year is
due to the fact, which I have noticed, that
a pair of badgers do not breed every year.
I cannot decide whether there is any precise
rule, but am inclined to think that they breed
once every two years. There are so many
accounts of single badgers kept in confinement
bringing forth young after a much longer
period of gestation that it appears possible
that the female has the power known to be
possessed by the Roe-deer doe of postponing
the operation of parturition for a considerable
time.

The badger is not by nature a ferocious animal, though the female will repel with the greatest savagery any approach when she has young, but so will a hen with chickens. The temperament of the badger is a gentle, shrinking one. No animal prefers a more quiet life, loving a warm bed in a dry dark corner of earth or rocks. He loves to sleep and meditate in peace for the greater part of the twenty-four hours. He lies not far within his entrance hall during the spring and summer, and on a hot day he will sometimes come to the mouth of his hole. In the evening, in June or July, he will come outside, sit looking into the wood or shuffle round the bushes, stretch himself against the tree-stems, or have a clumsy romp with his wife and little ones; and when the daylight dies he will hurry off, rushing through the covert for his nightly ramble. In the summer months he will travel as far as six miles from home, but he is in bed again an hour before sunrise.

It is only at this time of the year that he can be hunted above ground. This can be

done with a few beagles or harriers on a moonlight night, when, finding him in the open,
they will give a merry chase and fine cry,
and a run of several miles without a check.
If his earths are stopped, and he finds no
other refuge, he will be brought to bay. In
some districts I have known sacks put into
the mouths of the most used holes of a set,
the open end of each sack having a running
noose pegged into the ground, thus providing
an astonishing reception on his return as he
charges in, disturbed or pursued in his mid-
night ramble. By this means he is taken
alive and unhurt, being bagged and secured
in his attempt to enter. At other times of
the year, when the days are short and the
nights longer, he comes out later in the
evening, waits for a moment at the mouth
of his earth, takes a preliminary sniff round,
and then rushes off at the top speed into the
covert.

The badger is easily domesticated if
brought up by hand, and proves an interesting and charming companion. I had at
one time two that I could do anything with,

and which followed me so closely that they would bump against my boots each step I took, and come and snuggle in under my coat when I sat down. I was very much attached to them, but having to leave for the London season, I came home after a prolonged absence to find that they had reverted to their natural disposition, and had forgotten him who had been a foster-parent to them. As I could not fondle them without a pair of hedging-gloves on, and they no longer walked at my heel, I made them a home in the woods, where the thought of their happiness has helped me to bear my loss.

Many interesting stories are told of tame badgers. Here is one taken from the *Field:* "A few months ago, a farmer in the Cotswolds unearthed a badger and one youngster about two months old, which were sent to Mr. Barry Burge, Northleach, who only kept the former a few weeks, when she died. The orphan was petted very much by its owner. In a short time it would follow Mr. Burge through the fields and streets, and answer to the call like a dog. It is an amusing sight to see the badger along with its master riding a bicycle. A short time ago Mr. Burge had a fox cub, which he has succeeded in taming. This fox has taken a great fancy to an Irish terrier, with which she plays continually. The badger, which is now about seven months old, is loose about the house at times, but generally spends most of its time in company with the fox, to which it is greatly attached, all sleeping snugly together."—G. W. Duckett, Northleach, R.S.O., Gloucestershire.

M. le Masson gives a pretty account of his tame badger, which, though it loses much in translation, I give in English. " I brought up and kept for more than two years a female badger, which died at last from obesity. She had been taken from her mother when only eight days old and suckled by a Normandy bitch, which had already reared me some wolf whelps. 'Grisette,' as she was named, was, like all her kind, omnivorous; meat, beetles, fruits, certain kinds of vegetables, in fact, all and everything was welcome to her healthy appetite. When out walking in the country, where she always readily followed me, she would unearth rats, moles, and young rabbits, which she could scent at the bottom of their holes. In spite of her thorough domesticity, I never succeeded in overcoming her antipathy to dogs, and more especially to cats, which she chased most viciously did they dare to enter the kitchen where she reigned as queen; and where, such was her sensitiveness to cold, she had made her bed against the wall in the chimney corner. Here in winter, buried in her furs, she slept curled up for whole days together. But which of us is without a fault? A little greedy without being actually voracious, sweet Grisette sometimes ventured on to the stone-work of the cooking-stove, and from there was able to discover from which of the saucepans was exhaled the most savoury odour, and never did she make a mistake on that score!"

Du Fouilloux states in his *Venerie*:—"Je ay veu aux blereaux prendre deuant moy les petis cochons de laict, lesquelz ilz traynoient tout vifz en leur terrier. C'est vne chose certaine qu'ilz en sont plus friandz que de toutes autres chairs : car si on passe vn carnage de porceau par dessus leurs terriers, ilz ne faudront iamais de sorter pour y aller."

The badger is credited with a special love for pork. I have seen a statement in an old volume of the *Gentleman's Recreation*, in which the writer refers to the taste of the badger for pork. "They love Hog's-flesh above any other ; for take but a piece of Pork and train it over a badger's Burrow, if he be within, you shall quickly see him appear without."

Badgers are omnivorous. In their wild state their food is principally roots and insects —they are especially fond of beetles and such creatures as are to be found just below the surface of the ground, or under the decaying dung of cattle. The natural history books say they eat frogs. This may be true, but I have not observed it. I have tried badgers in confinement with all sorts of insects and grubs, but I never could get them to touch slugs or worms. They are carnivorous, and eat mice, rats, voles, and moles. They will take a rabbit out of a trap, turn it inside out, and eat all the meat, leaving the skin behind, turned neatly with the fur inside. They are also fond of very young rabbits, and will dig a shaft through several feet of solid earth direct on to the nest. But when this has been stated, nearly all has been said with regard to their propensity to damage in game coverts. I am supported by other observers in this opinion; for. instance, a recent writer in the *Field* who says :—"In reply to E. T. D'Egmont's inquiry about catching badgers, I have never found them do much harm to the nests of winged game ; but they are death on rabbits, and much resemble a fox in finding a young one appetizing. Their skins would make good waistcoats, but, apart from that, I would not destroy them upon any property of my own, because they do so much more good than harm in divers ways. We have a small property in my family, where foxes and badgers lie up together in close proximity to a rabbit warren, upon the inhabitants of which they feed. It is a spot practically unknown to the outward gaze of man, as it is difficult of access; and I should fancy that any one attempting to attack their stronghold would meet with a stubborn resistance. Badgers mostly go seeking for food during the night-time. Where they abound, one occasionally meets them walking quietly along a path, with their snout low down, and occasionally giving a kind of grunt like a mongoose. They are very fond of honey. A bag pegged back over the entrance to their holes is a good way of catching them."

They do not hunt for rabbits or game like a fox or cat, and though there are undoubtedly instances of their taking partridge and pheasant eggs, in my experience I have never known it done by those around me, nor from other places where they have ample opportunity of doing so. I have known a pheasant rear a young brood on an earth tenanted by badgers; but, curiously enough, I have known a similar case on a fox's earth, containing a vixen and cubs, and I cannot defend the general character of a fox in regard to game. Still it may be taken that a badger, though occasionally eating rabbits and rarely eggs, does not hunt for game, ground or feathered, or do a hundredth part of the damage done by a fox or a cat. There have always been more rabbits, hares, and pheasants in a hollow near my house, where there is a large colony of badgers, than in any other part of the coverts. The badger has a special weakness for wild honey, and the grubs of wasps and humble bees. The wildest and most unconciliatory badgers I have ever had in confinement would come out and eat a wasp's nest, and they will hunt every bank and hedgerow in July and August, routing out every wasp's and hornet's nest in the country-side. A keeper told me that upon one occasion, when he was walking along the covert edges in summer-time about nine o'clock in the evening, his attention was arrested by a curious chapping, champing noise, and looking over the fence he saw an old badger with his head in a huge wasp's nest hanging in a bramble bush, and he was

crunching up and eating with the greatest
gusto the wasps and grubs, quite undeterred
by the thousand angry insects that covered
his head and body. In truth, I must admit
that while he is thus useful, he has been
known to enter a garden and upset the hives
and purloin the honey, being as fond of it as
his larger cousins, the bears.

I must also bring another charge against
him. Let me introduce this painful subject
by giving the following correspondence from
the *Field* newspaper :—

" Wilfred writes—' I shall be obliged if
you will allow me to ask your readers whether
they have known old badgers to kill fox
cubs. Last year our M.F.H. gave a neighbouring keeper a litter of cubs. He put them
into a natural empty fox-earth, and kept them
shut in until they had got fairly on their
feed, and were quite at home. When he
opened the earth, and allowed them to
come out, they played about, and all went
well for two or three days, when he found
one at a little distance from the mouth of
the earth dead, with its skull smashed in,

and very much bitten about the head and neck. He lost the lot in the same way in a few days. He thought an old badger or fox killed his cubs. About this time I got five cubs, and put them into an empty artificial fox-earth. All went well with them for some time after they played out, when the keeper reported finding one about twenty yards from the earth dead, and killed after the same fashion as my neighbour's cubs, and I too lost mine. In the same artificial earth I had a natural litter this season, and the cubs played out well; but on the keeper telling me he did not think they were there now, I went to examine the earth, found the foxes gone, and the earth occupied by an old badger. I had a litter of fox cubs in the deer park here, where I live, and all went well with them until ten days ago, when one was picked up dead, killed in the same manner as those last year, and another was found dead yesterday. I feel quite certain myself that they were killed by an old badger or an old fox, for I am sure if killed by dogs they would not smash the skull and neck. I shall be glad if any one can enlighten me on this subject.' "

In reply to " Wilfred " there were several letters, among which were the following :—

" Sir,—Undoubtedly; every one that they can get near, and more especially hand-reared cubs that have not got the old foxes to protect them. I was first told this by old Jem Hills, the well-known huntsman of the Heythrop, in his latter years ; and subsequently I had positive proof of what he said. On one occasion a man brought a fine half-grown cub to my house which he had picked up dead in the road he came along. It was bitten most severely through and behind the shoulder, and I at once remarked to a friend that was with me, 'That is the work of a badger.' On going down to an earth where I knew there was a natural litter, we found tracks of a badger all about the place, as if he had been hunting the cubs. Having at the time eight cubs that I was hand-rearing in an artificial drain, I thought it was high time to look after them, for though regularly fed, I did not always watch to see whether they all came to feed. However, I did so that evening, and only two came, and these looked very wild and scared. I then searched the plantation, and picked up four of my cubs killed quite recently, and bitten in the same savage way. A few weeks after we killed a big boar badger in the drain. Several years later, I was again rearing some hand-bred cubs, and everything went well until they were a good size, when one morning I found one of them killed, evidently by a badger ; and I eventually took four more of them, and the others were all driven away. This badger beat me for some little time, but I got him at last. Though old badgers and foxes are often found in the same earth, more frequently when one of the latter has been run to ground by hounds, yet, as a rule, they give each other wide berths. If your correspondent · 'Wilfred' wishes to save his cubs, let him kill every badger as soon as possible."

" Sir,—Replying to 'Wilfred's' question, 'Do badgers kill fox cubs?' I cannot say they do, because there are no badgers in this district ; but having at different times had young foxes killed in the way he describes, namely, bitten in the head, I can assure him that it is done by an old dog fox. Should he wish for further information, I refer him to Mr. John Douglas, Royal Hotel, Pudding Chare, Newcastle-on-Tyne, who will tell him of the experience he gained when at Clumber, under the Duke of Newcastle."

" Sir,—I may tell 'Wilfred' that I have never known old badgers kill fox cubs, though I have studied the habits of both for nearly forty years. No doubt an old vixen, with no cubs of her own, killed his ; the dog fox will not do this. Indeed, he will cater for all the cubs of his own get, but a strange vixen is very apt to kill any cubs which have no mother of their own. I have known a terrier bitch kill a litter of foxhound puppies, and one of my Irish terriers will kill puppies if she has the chance. As to the 'natural' litter

which 'Wilfred' found gone, they had merely
been shifted by the vixen; as soon as the
cubs get able to travel they are always shifted.
Last year I had two tame wild ducks sitting in
a hedge. A badger passed regularly within
a yard of them every night, but they were
undisturbed. This year a fox took one of
them just before it hatched. I was sorry to
read the other day in the *Field* an account of
two old and four cub badgers having been
dug out in Gloucestershire. There is surely
no sport in this, and the badgers are destitute
of grease now, whereas at Michaelmas they
are fat enough to provide grease for all the
rheumatic people in the parish. I like to
catch one with my terriers when the harvest
moon shines. Sometimes I get up in a con-
venient tree near the earth and watch the
badgers feeding on the crazy roots. How
fond they are of the wild bees' honey, and
also of wasps' nests. Let me advise
'Wilfred' to read the exhaustive and interesting account given in a letter to the *Times*
(October 24, 1877), and quoted in *Cassell's
Natural History*, vol. ii. It thus concludes—

'The badgers and the foxes are not unfriendly, and last spring a litter of cubs was brought forth very near the badgers ; but their mother removed them after they had grown familiar, as she probably thought they were showing themselves more than was prudent.' Mr. Ellis of Loughborough was the author of the letter, and he had rare opportunities of studying the habits of badgers."

I am loth to do it, but wishing to be an impartial historian, am compelled to state that the badger is capable of vulpicide. As a rule he can put up with an occasional lodger of the fox family, and live happily with him, and from his superior qualities as an architect of subterranean dwellings, he is on the whole an encourager of foxes. He often gives up his spacious apartments to a vixen in the spring, and submits to eviction. A fox will often take possession of a badger's earth, new or old ; and in order to persuade foxes to take to a particular covert, no surer method can be pursued than to get badgers to make earths when they are required. But even a badger's patience can be exhausted, as the following history of my own experience will show. I would premise, however, that I do not credit the oft-repeated story that the fox gets rid of the badger by leaving his evacuations in the badger's earth. Being the less and weaker animal, all a fox does is allowed on sufferance. My suspicions of a badger's capability to wage war on foxes were first aroused some years ago. The badgers had made a fine double set of earths on the north side of a hill in a neighbouring larch wood, where no effort on my part to get foxes to breed and stay had succeeded. No sooner, however, was a colony of badgers established than foxes haunted the holes and covert. In a succession of years there was as certain to be a litter of fox cubs in the badger earth as a sunrise on the morrow.

What happened each spring was that the foxes and badgers frequented both sets indiscriminately till about March. When the vixen lay in the badgers abandoned the set of holes where she was, and restricted themselves to the other set some twenty yards

distant.  Year after year the fox cubs pros-
pered and grew up, till one summer the keeper
found a fox cub in a field with his head bitten
in two and terribly worried.  I did not know
how to account for it.  I watched the vixen
and the other cubs one evening to see that
they were all right, and saw them, but found
they had left the earth and were in the
covert.  For two years all went well and the
foxes were unmolested, and then occurred
something that gave me a clue to the death
of the cub three years before  Two vixens lay
in at the badgers' earth, and brought up their
families of seven and four respectively, till
they were about one-third grown.  There
were then to my knowledge at least four
badgers and twelve foxes in these two earths.
On one or two occasions the stillness of the
night was broken by the veriest pandemonium
at the earth, but still I did not think much
of it.  At the end of the hunting season, at
the end of April, when the cubs were seven
or eight weeks old, and a fortnight after the
hounds had been through the coverts, I found
the largest and finest of the vixens dead, and

thought that, in spite of the earths being open, she must have been chopped by the hounds. A post-mortem examination, as well as the improbability of a vixen with cubs being out in the early part of the day, convinced me that she had not been killed by hounds. She seemed to have been badly bitten through the legs and thighs but not on the body. From this time the other vixen and all the cubs left the badgers' earths and remained in the covert. It was on this occasion that an attempt to find out how many badgers there were in these earths was rewarded by seeing seven full-grown badgers emerge from a single hole. It was rough, no doubt, that the badgers should be invaded by two large families of smelling foxes, and no doubt their patience had become exhausted. Still I could not tolerate this kind of behaviour, and so I had a dig at them, took two old ones out, and transported them to Scotland. The following year there was peace and fox cubs again. The year after, however, the vixen and her cubs took off into the covert very early after another bit of Bank Holiday

business, at a time of night when all respect-
able people were quietly in bed. And yet all
through the year foxes are in the earth, and
this spring, as heretofore, a litter of cubs
has been raised, but removed to another
earth at a safe distance from the badgers. I
have never heard of badgers taking the offensive against foxes; they will never molest a
fox or vixen unless their earth is invaded, and
in my case if I had had no badgers in this
covert I should have had no foxes; and whilst
it is annoying that the fox cubs and vixen
should be driven out, and perhaps occasionally
killed, the drawback is slight when it is
considered that as long as there are badgers there will be a litter of cubs, which nine
times out of ten will get safely off.

There are every now and then albino badgers reported, but I have never seen one
alive. I think, however, they are more
subject to albinism than most animals. I
do not know of a case of melanism.

"*White Badger at Overton, Hants.*—
While digging for badgers on April 30, we
came across two dog badgers in the same

earth, one of which was quite white, the colour of a white ferret, with pink eyes. Unfortunately, the terriers punished him so much he had to be destroyed. I have helped to dig out a great many of these animals, but never saw nor heard of a white one before."
—T. P.

# PART III

THERE are several methods by which the badger can be taken alive, or killed, with ease. I am familiar with several successful ways of trapping him. The reader, if he is not aware of these, must not expect me to enlighten him, as my object in writing is to arouse an interest in his preservation, not to facilitate his destruction. It may be as well to state, however, that the inhuman engine, the steel trap (by which so many of the birds and beasts that frequented the wild woods of England and Scotland have been exterminated) is an instrument that arouses the suspicion of a badger at once, and he is as clever in avoiding it as an old-fashioned rat. The badger if caught in a steel trap will frequently bite his leg or foot clean off. In my opinion there are two legitimate methods of hunting the badger. First, that of a straight-forward attack on his fortress; and should it be an old-established earth, it may be the end of the longest day will not see the battle ended. There are, of course, the fortunes of war—a lucky engagement, a wrong turn on the part of the defender, a successful trench quickly cutting off his retreat—which may deliver him unexpectedly into your hands; or the enemy may outwit you altogether, conducting a masterful retreat, with gallant sorties on the dogs, and by continually changing his front drive you to abandon works, trenches, and operations that have cost great labour and time; thus you may be left with a tired and wounded pack of terriers, exhausted sappers, and the badger, having blocked and barricaded his retreat with soil, stones, and sand, is lost. The war thus made is an equal one : you attack him on his own ground in his fortress where he is acquainted with every passage, gallery, and casement; he is armed to the teeth and armour-plated, and can drive a road forward, downward, or upward with extra-ordinary rapidity. It is true you may have many terriers, but he has an advantage over your forces. Only one of your dogs can engage at a time, and the badger has the advantage of weight, size, knowledge of the ground, and familiarity with the dark—in fact, in every respect except those of courage and endurance, which in some terriers may equal his own. The other method, less sure, depends on taking the badger off his guard, and is more in the character of an ambuscade under cover of night. When the badgers are away from home you block up their earths, placing sacks with running nooses in the mouth, in the most frequented holes. Station one of your party near the "set," and you may either take a small pack of hounds and draw the country for a few miles round, and hunt him like a fox, getting a run across country and a fine cry ; or you may beat the neighbouring coverts with men and dogs of any description that are trained to hunt the badger.

In the following, taken from an article

which appeared in a newspaper, there is a good account of night hunting.

"Owing to his shy and retiring habits, rather than to the scarcity of the animal, probably less is known about the badger than about any wild animal left in England at the present time. There is a prevalent notion that the badger is exceedingly rare, and also that he is harmless; neither of these ideas is quite correct. In the west especially the badger is fairly common, but escapes notice owing to his retiring disposition. Whether he does harm to feathered game or not is a moot point, but his tracks have been distinctly noticed round plundered nests; it is certain, however, that he does great damage to ground game by digging out 'stops' of young rabbits in the spring and summer.

"When hunted after the fashion generally adopted in the west, he affords excellent sport to those who are prepared to face a long tramp and the loss of some of their night's rest. The prosaic way of digging them out of the earth involves much labour, and has in it no element of sport; while

attempting to catch badgers in traps is about
as feasible as trying to catch birds by putting
salt on their tails. Driving them into sacks
fixed in the earth is unsatisfactory, as a good
game dog is necessary to press the badger
hard, or he will turn from the earth and seek
shelter elsewhere ; while, if you have a good
dog, the sacks are unnecessary except for the
reception of the badger when caught by the
dog.

"The paraphernalia of the chase are
simple, namely, a good dog, a pair of badger-
tongs, and a sack. A really good dog is
very difficult to obtain ; the favourite kind is
a cross-bred bull-terrier, about forty pounds
in weight; pure-bred bull-terriers, for some
reason or other, do not seem to give satisfaction. The 'tongs' have wooden handles,
and iron heads with blunt teeth for grasping
the badger when held by the dog. For a
successful hunt it is necessary to observe
which way the badger travels from the
earth. A favourite spot is the slope of a hill,
or high-lying fields, where they may be easily
tracked by the 'roots,' i. e. small holes

which they scratch in the ground in search of beetles and roots of various kinds. They rarely descend into low-lying meadows, except to drink. Choose a starlight night with a slight breeze blowing, and approach the earth up the wind. Do not hurry your dog; if he knows his work, he will range freely, but he often takes a long time to puzzle out the track. If you miss him, go on slowly in the direction in which you last saw him, often stopping to listen.

"'What was that?' The dry sticks crack in a hedge far below you. 'Hark! two sharp eager barks; what does it mean?' Why, that Grip is wheeling out in a half-circle to gain slightly on the badger, and then to dash in and get him by the head. Run now as you never ran before. Head over heels into a ditch; never mind, up and on again—the best dog can't hold a badger for ever. There they are out in the open, Grip with a tight hold of the badger by the side of the head, with his legs tucked back out of harm's way. Grasp him with the tongs as near the neck as possible. Take off the dog, some one. Hold the bag. Hoist our grey-coated friend into the air, and lower him into the sack ; he weighs at least thirty pounds. The dog is hardly marked, and you haven't torn more than three rents in your nether garments getting through that last thorn hedge. Altogether, every one agrees that it was a satisfactory little run.

" The old English sheep-dog I have known do well for the other method. The badger when pursued makes straight for home, blunders headlong into the hole, only to find that his efforts to get in are closing the mouth of the sack, that retreat or fighting are alike in vain, and that he is an imprisoned bagman, without having struck a blow in self-defence. It is not uncommon for a badger thus pursued to stand at bay, when a good dog may keep him in play, or hold on, till you come up and secure him. No doubt there is amusement and excitement in this moonlight chase, and to some it is preferable to the arduous labour with pick, spade, axe, and terrier."

To my mind, however, there is something more interesting and exciting in the long-

sustained conflict and labour of the latter, for
which you require perseverance, wit, patience,
and courage on the part of man and terrier.
The courage and endurance that a good terrier
will display when need requires before such a
foe, will fill his owner's heart with joy and
pride. A good terrier is a veritable treasure;
the price of a sure, game, and determined
one is far above rubies. Picture what it
means for a small terrier to enter into the
bowels of the earth to find, to cope with, and
for long hours in dust and darkness in the
tortuous maze to keep up an unequal fight
with an enormously superior foe, whose
grunts and clattering teeth add terror to his
charges down the echoing ways. Yet I have
had not a few that, hour after hour, on their
backs or their sides, would lie up to a badger,
keeping him cornered, and continuously give
tongue with no voice to direct them. Should
the badger charge, such a terrier would
rather die than let him leave the corner to
which he has been driven, and will return
fighting and facing his huge opponent, driving him inch by inch into the *cul de sac*,

caring neither for bite nor wounds, and
making noise enough to let you know where
the battle rages.  It is no part of his duty to
tackle the badger.  A good terrier knows
this, and will only resort to his teeth should
the badger attempt to force a passage.  If it
comes to close quarters, such a terrier will
draw back his fore-legs under his body, take
the attack full in the face, and trust to seizing
the badger by the neck.  A badger when
attacked generally bites upwards, *i. e.* he
lowers his head and turns the back of his
head downwards.  Nothing makes the heart
beat faster than, with head to the earth, to
hear the din of this subterranean warfare
carried along the dark galleries to the day.
You have sent in one of your best terriers ;
he has tried by cajolery and caresses, by
cries, by straining at his chain to be allowed
the honourable distinction of first blood.
You have dispatched him with your blessing,
and he has quickly and silently started on his
journey into the unknown.  You listen to
him forcing his passage, drawing himself round
corners, scratching away some accumulation

or fall from the roof, and hear his eager panting as he winds his foe. Presently you hear a low sharp bark, then another, then two or three more, next a bumping, thumping noise; it is the badger, who has waited to see who the intruder is, and, rousing himself, is retreating. The terrier barks no more, but you can hear the thump-thump of the badger, followed by the efforts of the dog to keep up with him. They are now a long way in, and you can plainly hear the bark again. Soon the fight draws nearer, and the terrier's cry comes to your ear with regularity and clearness; but the badger is only disputing the way, he has not yet been driven with his back against the wall. The terrier redoubles his activity, you can hear him feinting at the badger, sharp give-and-take, but no foolish attempt to lay hold. After ten minutes the badger again retreats, probably up the hill, and you have to listen on the surface or at the higher holes of the set till you can hear them again. At last you catch a faint sound, they are still moving, now stationary, now further on; then they seem to stay in one place. There is the steady yap-yap-yap of the dog just distinguishable to the ear.

Quick, every hand to work. A trench six feet deep, or deeper if necessary, must be cut across the set to cut off the badger from the passages. With pick, spade, and shovel the work goes on, while some one listens to know whether the scene of battle moves. If it does, the badger may have found a side gallery, and gone far enough, or he may have charged the dog. He may have passed by a different road beneath your feet in the trench; but if the terrier has succeeded in keeping him face to face and engaged, yet not driving him so hard as to make him charge, you may be successful in an hour or two, and find that your cutting intersects the passage in which the badger and the terrier are engaged. If the badger suspects you are cutting off his only means of escape he will charge and fight, and the terrier will sometimes be unable to back fast enough; then there will be a meeting of teeth and jaws, the badger holding the dog through the head, jaw, or nose. The dog's smothered cries of anger and pain make you strain every nerve to get to his relief.

When the badger at last leaves go, the terrier's turn comes, and now with blood up he drives back the badger to his end of the hole with every determination to keep him there. After two or three turns like this, if the dog has been in an hour or two, he will probably come out for a breath of air for a moment. He should be immediately taken, fastened up, watered, and kept in reserve for future contingencies, and the best terrier for sticking up be sent in with the utmost haste. If a minute has been spent in doing this, every moment will have been used by the badger in barricading the passage against the dog and burying himself. This once accomplished, you may as well whistle for your badger as continue digging, for he may have got down into some other gallery, or have buried himself so that neither dog nor man can find him. Of one thing you may be sure, that whilst you are speculating what has become of him, he is digging at a prodigious rate, or has already made his escape by some secret stair.

If, however, you are quick, terrier number two has interrupted master badger as he is at work and lets you know. "It's all right," "Come on," "He's here," "I've got him," "He's got me," "You beast," "Get back," "I'll hold him," and spade and shovel and pick are hard at work again. Backs and arms are aching with lifting at high pressure out of the deep trench. You dig on, blocking the hole as the roof falls in, but every now and then the shovels clear it for a moment to give the dog air. And now the game has shown itself. A terrible charge down the hole sends out the terrier; and the badger, seeing the men at work, backs again, followed by the dog. Now all is excitement. Every snap, haunch, grunt, groan, and yell in the fight is heard. A favourite's life in the balance! The prize in view! The other terriers are tugging at their chains, frantic to join the fray, yelling fit to split their throats. It is maddening for them to see the dust and commotion in the trench, to hear the sound of battle so near, to wind the enemy, to hear the cry of their fighting and perhaps wounded companion, and not to be allowed to share in the glory of the final action. Now is the time if you have a terrier to enter to see what he is made of, but there is no time to waste on education. You are close up to the badger, he cannot be an arm's-length off. Draw your dog, the badger will then turn his tail to you to dig, or he will charge out. Be ready with the tongs, and a good dog in case he charges. But if he turns tail get hold of it with a good grip. A long pull and a steady pull will draw him out, bouncing, lunging, and snapping. Now, boys, ready with the sack! Dogs off. All want steady nerves now; three hands on the sack mouth to keep it open, and take care of your fingers! A twirl round and a quick plunge, and the badger is in the bag. Don't let go his tail till you have slipped the cord on his hind-leg, and made the other end of the cord fast to the bag mouth and to a tree. I have seen a badger go through a sack like a bullet through paper, and it is well to make all as safe as possible.

M. Edmond le Masson, in his book on hunting fox and badger, severely deprecates tailing a badger. He denounces the danger and folly of it, and gives an amusing account of his falling into a trench at the critical moment as follows :—

"One fine day, or rather one cursed day, when I was sweating blood and water to get a monster badger out of his earth, a venerable patriarch, white with years, who resisted my aching tired arms and weary back with all his strength, the earth gave way and I fell back, rolling over with the animal, and there I was at the bottom of the abyss in a veritable pandemonium. Bruised and breathless, I was conscious enough to know that I was in very bad company, with four more badgers, a furious mother and three young ones, and not so young either but that one of them was able to tear from me a large piece of the most indispensable part of my attire, which placed me in a position of cruel embarrassment, and obliged me to wait till the shades of night enabled me to get home with decency. The most humiliating part of the adventure was that all these cursed brutes, father, mother, and children, made the most insolent retreat over my stomach to escape from their earth, and then took off straight across country and escaped. From this moment I have felt a ferocious malice against all badgers, whether big, middling, or little, and I never go down into the trench now without having a Lefaucheux revolver and a Devisme revolver, a long dagger knife, and a sharp Toledo colichemarde!"

But let not ingenuous youth think that to enjoy the sport all he has to do is to take a spade and any reputable terrier. He might as well try, like Dame Partington, to stop the rising tide with a mop! Before so serious an enterprise as a badger digging be undertaken, the wise man will see to it that all the materials are ready, and let him be sure that he has the first necessity—the stout heart to go through with a tough job when once started. I have, with my brother, Mr. J. A. Pease, started at 7.30 a.m. from home, worked a summer's day with a slight refreshment at one, handled pick and shovel and spade, fought the terriers, and gone on through the afternoon, evening, and a black wet night, without even a drop of water to slake our parched throats, deserted by all but one faithful workman, and on till the grey dawn of another day, which found us as weary, wet, and wounded, and as disreputable a looking company of three men and four terriers as ever survived a bloody action. At five o'clock we secured a splendid pair of badgers, which we bore home on aching backs, followed by our gallant little team of draggled and dirty terriers. On another occasion, it took my brother and myself, some ten labourers and keepers, and nine terriers, from 10 till 5.30 to take an old 30-lb. dog badger, in an earth which had only one hole, and where it was a case of following straight into the hill. It is wonderful what can be done by twelve men with pick, spade, and shovel in seven hours. On this occasion we dug a trench ten feet long into the hill, and then the depth of bearing necessitated our making a drift, or tunnel, which we drove in thirty feet. The heat and want of air inside made the work difficult. Candles would not burn after we had gone about twenty feet, and the tunnel was so low that we had to work on our knees and then on our stomachs. There was a considerable danger from the roof falling in, but the fight waged so fiercely that we thought of little but what was ahead of us. When at last we got within distance of the badger, he was in rocky ground, we could mine no further, and being on a shelf round a corner no terrier could draw him. As I was the smallest of the party, it fell to me to try and reach him, and I crawled up as far as I could, holding a little bull-terrier on whom I could rely for protection for my face, and a pair of short badger tongs. I had indeed a bad quarter of an hour!

It was stifling, cramped, and pitch dark. I kept the terrier in front of my head and gallantly he behaved, though every now and then the badger's charge, or a fierce encounter, nearly smothered me with dust and soil, against which I could not protect myself, as I was powerless to retreat, there being only room to lie flat on the ground. The man behind me was in the same position, tight hold of my ankles, and the man again behind him, and the rest of the force made a human chain, which on a signal from me was to be drawn out to daylight. Many attempts I made when the badger charged to get him with the tongs, but I had so little room to work my hands in that I missed him, and heard and felt the click and snack of his teeth on the iron. At last I felt I had hold of something, and I slipped the guard on the tongs, making the hold sure. I cried " Haul away," holding the terrier with one hand between me and the badger, and the tongs in the other. I found that he came with wonderful ease. It was not till we got to the light that I saw I had the huge bouncing brute by one claw, " Nip " diverting his attention from my head and hands. The labourers set up a shout, " He's got him by the clee," and a minute later we had the satisfaction of bagging him. But we were out only

just in time. I had gone back with the
terriers to see if there was nothing more in,
and hardly had got outside again, when there
was a fall from the roof that would, if it had
taken place earlier, have buried some of us
alive. As it was I looked round to see if we
were all there. The men were, but one little
terrier, " Pepper," a real treasure belonging
to a neighbour of mine in Cleveland, Mr. J.
P. Petch, was missing. We went in and
found him buried, but got him out alive and
little the worse. This was the biggest badger
my brother and I ever got.

But these operations are quite surpassed
by those M. le Masson related in the
following authentic story.

"An extraordinary *chasse* that lasted without
interruption three days and three nights, took
place lately in the neighbourhood of St.
Omer, on some land in the picturesque com-
mune of Wisques, in a wood attached to
the château of Madame la douairière Cauvet
de Blanchonval.

"One morning two young sportsmen of
St. Omer, MM. Théobald Cauvet and

Charles d'Hallewyn, were told by the *garde forestier* that on his beat he knew of several badgers near the place they call l'Ermitage.

"The little dogs being put on the scent soon found the earths, where they entered, and advanced with so much courage that they never stopped till they had reached the bottom of the earth, where they cornered the badgers, which held their ground in an attitude of the most threatening defence.

"The assailants, thus powerless, made themselves heard by barking and baying incessantly, and with heroic pluck, the little fellows refused to retreat in spite of the repeated calls of their masters.

"Their perseverance being carried to this length, our young gentlemen formed a resolution worthy of their taste for great undertakings and adventures. Labourers were called from the field and commissioned at once to set to work to reach the badgers.

"The attempt was more than bold. The mouths of the set, three in number, were at the foot of a hill, and embraced between them a sort of triangular piece of land at the apex of which the passages all united and formed a single underground gallery. The dogs having each entered by a separate hole made this clear.

"A shaft was sunk in order to start a tunnel at the opening of the lowest hole, but a depth of 7 to 8 metres (23 to 26 feet) had to be sunk before the passage was reached; thence they followed the direction taken by the dogs, and enlarged the tunnel to reach them, making an underground roadway 5 feet high ($1\frac{1}{2}$ metres) and nearly 6 feet wide ($1\frac{3}{4}$ metres).

"Whilst the workmen were mining, the badgers on their part were also working ceaselessly, and kept blocking the road with the earth they threw back in front of the men who were pursuing them, whilst the latter worked in shifts (relieving parties). For three days and three nights these indomitable animals worked on, retreating all the time, during which they bored their way 49 feet whilst buried in this extension of their principal earth without air or food.

"At one time during this war *à outrance*

it was thought they had escaped by some means or other, but the game terriers, which had hardly left them since the beginning of the struggle, soon reassured the workers by their redoubled cries. The undertaking was pushed on with greater determination than ever, and when the tunnel had reached a length of more than 30 metres (100 feet) they came on three badgers, which were quickly popped into a sack by the keeper. One of them, however, in his struggles succeeded in escaping from the sack, and even tore the clothes of the man who was carrying him. MM. Cauvet and d'Hallewyn showed a persistent perseverance during the whole of this struggle. By day and by night each in turn directed the operations of a siege at which more than one other lover of the pleasures of the chase assisted."

I have given one or two out of many examples I could relate of the arduous nature of badger-hunting. Discipline among the workmen is as necessary as determination in every attempt to dig out badgers. Nothing imperils success so much as divided or disputed authority, and whilst every attention should be given to the opinions expressed in the councils of war during the progress of the siege, there must be no hesitation in carrying out the plan of campaign when once decided on, or the day may be wasted in earthworks, in making trenches, and attempts to cut off subterranean ways which have been begun only to be abandoned. The terriers are the most important requisite; they must be good, the right size, hardy, enduring, and reliable. No matter how game a dog is, if he cannot follow the badger he is useless. He must above all be full-mouthed, sharp-tongued, and ready to keep his voice going for hours together. He must be absolutely true, or he may make a fool of you, and lie fast in the earth baying an imaginary foe, or barking and scratching to get up a small rabbit-hole. Beware of a terrier that will think of such vermin when employed to fly at much higher game. They are worse indeed than useless, and often have I been driven nearly wild by being persuaded to allow some man proud of his terrier to let him go.

Nothing can be more exasperating than when, after several hours of heavy labour and straining effort, whilst the proud owner stands smiling by and boasting the merits of his nailing dog, you at length reach the scene of all the disturbance to see a dirty little brute scratching his feet to tatters, frothing at the mouth, and wow-wowing to get up a three-inch rabbit-hole.

An authority in the *Gentleman's Magazine* recommends collars of bells being attached to the terriers to make the badger bolt, and states that broad collars of badger-skin save their necks. The former I do not believe to be efficacious, as fire, smoke, and crackers will not make a badger bolt while any one is about, and if it were efficacious it would be very easy to lose a bolting badger. A collar on a terrier is more likely to hang a dog on a root end than to save him from a bite. A terrier ninety-nine times out of a hundred is bitten through the muzzle, under the jaws, and about the skull and ears, and when inexperienced, about the fore-legs and shoulders. I never saw a terrier badly bitten in the neck, though I have seen a terrier's side torn, and one that turned tail punished severely in the rear. Whilst the terrier for badger should be game to the death, it is all-important that he should mingle discretion with his valour, and not drive his superior foe to desperation, but content himself with keeping him at bay, only using his teeth at a pinch and in extreme cases. Tell me, reader, how many terriers you know who can or will go to ground, stay there, tell the truth always, pass through every place a badger can, keep his head under the most exasperating circumstances, and come up smiling and eager after every round, no matter how much punished?

What thousands of little curs there are called terriers, and fox-terriers that will no more go down a fox-earth than go up a chimney! How many thousands of the best of these, however finely shaped for the show-bench, that have no more idea of their profession and the duties for which nature made them, and from which they derive their name, than the man in the moon, and whose masters are satisfied if they can kill a few rats, and think them wonderfully game if they will tackle a cat!

From my boyhood I have had terriers, but I never thought one worth keeping that could not, or would not, go to ground and show himself or herself worthy of their honourable name. Appearance is nothing if the other qualities are not present. I have had a little wire-haired terrier bitch (with neat, golden-tanned ·marked head), pretty and gentle, and winning in all her ways, a companion that slept on my bed each night, and looked the picture of innocence lying by the hearth or even on a lady's lap; but within that bosom beat a courageous little heart, in her head throbbed a brain full of sagacious intelligence, and in that soft brown eye lurked hidden fire. She could give deep music long sustained, and she never winced before the enemy. I called her "Worry," a name that seemed most *mal à propos* to her casual acquaintance. For twelve long years she was at my side in all the ups and downs of life, leading the drag when I was at Cambridge, following foxhounds and bolting foxes when I was hunting, and my constant and daily companion, accompanying me into every county when I made an expedition against the badger. I was once amused by the remarks made about Worry by an old shoemaker who sometimes accompanied us with a good terrier when we were ratting. " Si' the (see thee), lads, Worry's t' yan (the one) fer (for) pickin' t' wick (the life) out on 'em," as she threw five or six big rats over her shoulder in half as many seconds. She died a terrible death, but game and uncomplaining to the last. She had a knack of squeezing herself through almost any kennel bars, and I had had to put her into a kennel for a time, and had the bars made narrower and covered with mesh wire netting. An hour after I had put her in I went to see her, and I was horror-struck to find that she was half through the bars nipped as in a vice, the wire torn with her teeth, and herself covered with blood and wounds, with one eye hanging out, blood flowing from her mouth, still fighting her way on—without a sound except her panting breath. She was delighted to see me, and with some trouble I liberated her, cut off her eye, staunched her wounds, and did all I could for her. She never even winced as I cut away the eye, and as she lay in her bed looked at me affectionately with her one eye and wagged her tail. · The following day, though she did not even whine, I saw she was in terrible pain ; and as she was at this time badly ruptured, and very lame owing to a carriage accident some years before which resulted in a broken thigh and a double fracture above the hock, I had her shot, and buried in a quiet corner of the orchard, with the inscription on her headstone "*Sit tibi terra levis.*"

The terriers I have found the best and surest are amongst the Yorkshire breed of hard, wire-haired fox-terriers, short in the leg and strong headed. All my own have been descended from a white, wire-haired terrier called Fuss, the best bitch I ever had, and a prize-winner. I bought her in 1870 or 1871 from a dealer called Wooton. She was bred by a man called Jack Ridd. Worry was out of

her.  My brother got a dog, Roger, a dead
game one, at the same time from the same
man, and nearly all the terriers I have had
since are descended from these two, with
out-crosses from local strains, including the
Rev. Jack Russell's blood.  I have seen
smooth-coated terriers do equally well, but
not often.  The former is a harder and more
enduring breed, though more difficult to keep
clean in the coat, and taking time to get
dry after wet in cold weather.  The endurance of the wire-haired is remarkable.  I
have now a terrier, bred through many lines
of my old favourites, which is twelve years
old.  His jolly face is scored with the marks
of a thousand fights with fox and badger,
and though lame in his shoulders, his eyes
dim with age, and crippled with rheumatism,
showing toothless gums when he smiles his
welcome, he has twice this summer found
alone the badger earths, and returned at
evening, each time with his score of marks
increased, and on the last occasion he left
one of his ears behind him![1]  A terrier that

[1] Dead since this was written.

will go off to a badger earth on his own
account, especially if a young one, will probably end his days and find his grave there.
I have known several do so. Poor old
Twig! Always happy, he seldom now
wanders further than the stable-yard, and
spends his declining days playing with the
foxhound pup or sleeping in the sun, when
in his dreams he fights his battles over again,
and thrice he slays the slain. When we were
young together he followed me every hunting morning to the meet, where he at once
incorporated himself with the pack, greeting
his friends in turn with a grin, a twist of his
body, and a wag of his stump ; and when the
daylight faded, and the horn sounded for
home, I had always to carry him off on my
saddle, so reluctant was he, after the longest
day, to leave his comrades of the chase.
This became so troublesome that at last I
yielded to the pressure of the huntsman, Will
Nicholl, who then hunted the Cleveland
hounds, to permit him to join the kennel
establishment. For three seasons he scarcely
missed a day, and when a fox was run to

ground, no matter after how long or fast a run,
the question, " Where is Twig?" was never
asked twice. . Always there when wanted,
always dependable and perfect at his work,
he shifted many a sulky fox that went to
ground. Then Will Nicholl went to the
Hurworth under Sir Reginald Graham, and
took Twig with him. He did two seasons in
the Hurworth country, from thence going to
the Burton with Nicholl again. After a
season there I had a letter saying that
Nicholl feared that the old dog would not
follow hounds another season, and he sent
him back with me. I summered him well;
he did the next season with the Cleveland,
and came out the following season when
hounds were handy or when occasion required, making eight seasons with foxhounds,
besides being hunted at badger in the summer
months. He had learnt not to be hard on a
fox, but I thought I detected him in an act
of violence something more than a year ago.
We had run to ground in a drain, and Twig,
who had heard hounds, had come across
country as fast as his old legs would carry .

him, and was in before I could say " Knife."
No sooner was he in than the fox was out,
with Twig at his brush. This was not at
all what we wanted, as the whole pack was
within fifteen yards. Twig collared the fox
as he bolted, and as the hounds were making
a dash at him. I was angry with Twig, lifted
the fox and Twig, who I thought was holding the fox, above my head to save reynard
from the hounds. Here I had to hold him
for five minutes, but when I tried to choke
the old dog off, I discovered that the fox was
holding Twig through the upper jaw, and
the dog was hanging with his whole weight
suspended on the fox's teeth. Having made
the fox leave go Twig fell to the ground, and
when all was clear I put the fox down, when
we had a sharp ten minutes to ground again.
I was there only just in time to prevent
Twig from going in to take his revenge—
the fox this time being left in peace. It is
as well to have with you one bull-terrier, or a
fox-terrier with a bit of bull about him. In
cases of emergency, and when close up, such
a dog comes in useful, but they are tiresome

brutes as a rule to do with; they get so excited that they do not care what they go at, it may be the dogs or yourself, or I have seen them set to worry a big stone. They often go to ground well, but have several faults. They *will* tackle the badger, get punished severely, and create all sorts of difficulties, and are generally nearly mute except when fighting.

I had a rare life of it on one expedition with a little bull-terrier called Nip that I bought from a Cornishman, after a long dig in which Nip had distinguished himself. He was a dirty white, ugly, undershot, crop-eared little brute, with a tail like a shaving-brush. Shy and nervous, he had a fiendish amount of pugnacity and pluck. When not otherwise employed, he wore his teeth to the gums in vain endeavours to get into the interior of large stones. In a railway-carriage, so delighted was he at all times to get to ground, that he would get under the seat, and refuse to be removed if he had not on a collar and chain, except with the badger-tongs. He had to be muzzled and chained when with other dogs, and even then would make an utter fool of himself in his attempts to fight on every occasion. He would, when he had lost a badger, sulk and refuse to come out, and as it was impossible to put in any other dog while he was there, he had to be dug to and drawn like a brock. Whilst at the end of a day, when every other animal had had more than enough, and was glad to get food and rest, he was ready to hold me by the leg, and it would take the tongs and a couple of men to get his collar on.

I have always had a great admiration for the short-coated, hard, Scotch terrier, and believe that they are admirably adapted for this chase, but I have had no experience of them. They seem cut out for it, being hardy, the right size, sharp-tongued, and amongst the most intelligent of the canine race. I knew of one who went to Craig Cluny in the edge of the Ballochbuie forest, and spent some hours in a vain attempt to dislodge a badger. He returned three miles to the inn at Braemar and found another terrier like himself; they trotted back together, and by their united efforts drew and killed an old badger! There is a spot near this place in the forest called Stra-na-brach—or the badger's crag—but the badger knows the place no more. The keeper has done his work with the trap throughout Aberdeenshire.

Dandie Dinmont no doubt bred his dogs from these terriers, but I have no belief that the present race is fitted for badger-hunting. Those one sees on a show bench are too large to get to ground quickly and easily, and I doubt if there is one of the race, as at present known, that has ever exchanged civilities with the badger in his natural earth. Dandie Dinmont bred his terriers for badgers, but I am sure his never were the size they are now; and although Sir Walter Scott has surrounded Dandie with a halo of interest, and made him immortal by his eulogies, his fiendish cruelties have always made me hate his name, and prejudiced me against a breed that was developed under a hideous system. It makes my blood boil to read of his terriers trained to face the badger by taking alive young and old badgers, and sawing off the under jaws, and employing other indescribably cruel methods.

The dachshund and the small basset, when properly selected, are splendidly adapted for badger-hunting. In Germany the former, and in France the latter, are generally bred for this purpose. Full-voiced and throwing a tongue like a hound, deep-chested, short-legged, and strong-bodied, they are perhaps the best one can have, but I do not think that they possess the endurance and quickness of an English terrier.

There was a breed of wire-haired black-and-tan English terriers, but I imagine them to be nearly, if not altogether, extinct, that from all accounts must have been really good terriers in the true meaning of the term.

In working dogs, be careful only to put in one at a time: you thus economize your forces, and avoid the risk of their fighting in the earth. More than this, if you let two dogs or a dog and a bitch in together, you subject them to danger and the probability of severe punishment. The dog in front is charged by the badger, the dog behind cares for nothing but that he may get to close quarters, and it is a case of those behind cry forward and those in front cry back. In such a position your terrier may have his legs and head broken, and be killed outright. Again, a good terrier works better and more steadily than with a companion, as the competition leads to jealousy. Put in your dog at the lowest or bottom hole of the set, driving the badger up-hill (or "to hill," as it is technically called) if you can. It is a much easier task to get a badger out in this manner, as the further up-hill the fewer are the passages, and generally speaking the nearer they lie to the surface. Furthermore, take care that you have a collar and chain for each dog, and that every terrier not on duty is securely fastened at a distance from the earth, and out of reach of any other dog.

The following are the requisite implements for badger digging; they should be good and handy tools :—

1 and 2. Spades. These should be handy,

and worn to that condition when the edge is sharp, and the tool works easily, without having lost its strength. They should vary but little from the ordinary garden or rabbit-

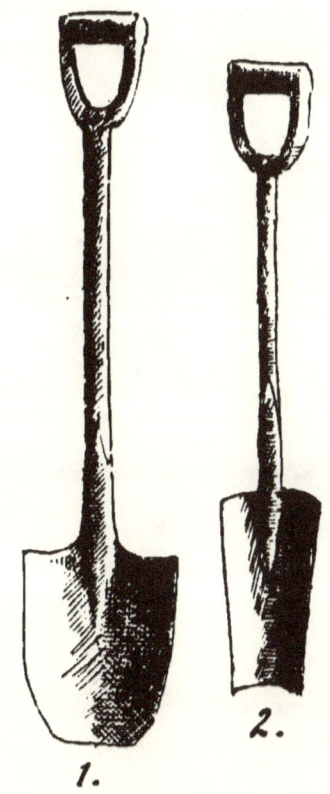

FIG. 7.

ing spade, except that where there is a depth of clay, and when in a deep trench, it may be easier or a relief to use a drainer's long narrow one.

3. A crowbar.

4. A scraper, or coal-rake.

5 and 6. Shovels, for clearing out the loose earth, including a short-handled one, or

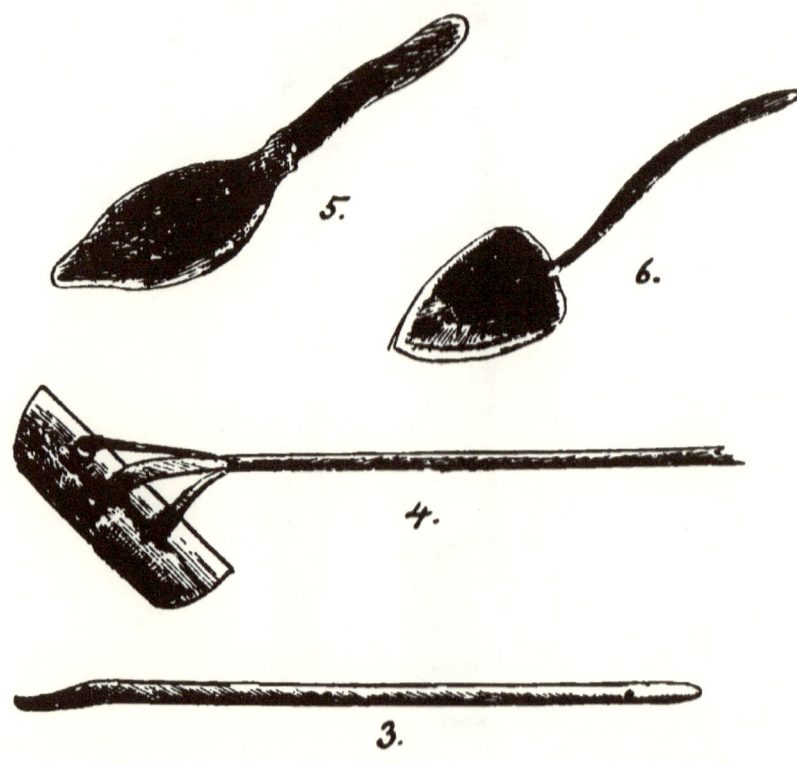

FIG. 8.

scoop, for opening the holes to let in air to the dogs.

7. An earth-piercer, in order to locate the fight.

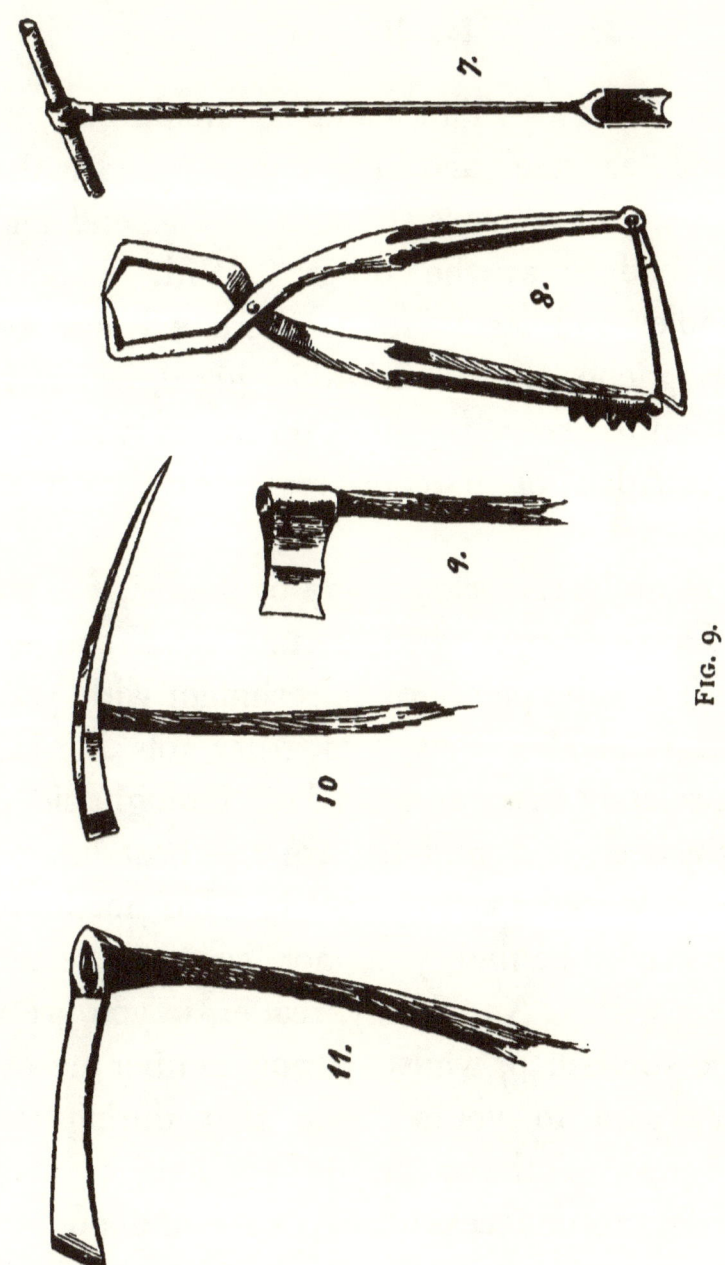

FIG. 9.

117

8. Tongs. The handles should be of wood, as steel and iron "give" under the pressure of a man's strength at one end and the badger at the other. With wooden handles and steel fittings there will still be spring enough to work the guard, which is put on to secure the hold on the animal.

9. Adze, or hatchet, for cutting roots of trees.

10 and 11. Picks, single or double.

Do not forget when starting on a badger-hunt to take plenty of refreshment with you, and remember that it is a dry job digging ceaselessly on a summer's day. Draught cider, light beer, and cold tea are the best liquors to work on for a long stretch. Do not leave the sacks behind you, nor cord to secure them with. And finally, reader, if you are a true sportsman, whilst sparing neither necessary pain to yourself nor dog during the progress of the siege, do not subject your terriers to unnecessary exposure and punishment; and when the day's work is done, however weary and however hungry you may be, do not attend to your own wants till you have seen each member of your gallant little pack well brushed and oiled (eyes and ears and wounds, if any, cleaned), fed, and put into a kennel with plenty of clean bedding. And do not forget to make a brave foe as comfortable as you can. If you keep a badger in confinement as a pet, he should have access to plenty of fresh cold water, and be fed on young rabbits and bread till accustomed to confinement, after which he will take gradually to and remain healthy on almost any scraps, meat, and vegetables from the house that you give him. He requires a dry dark kennel and yard, which should be kept scrupulously clean, when he will never be offensive. Some badgers take kindly at once to these new circumstances, others sulk and occasionally waste and die unless great care is taken. If the badger's evacuations show a tendency to purging, feed on bread chiefly and rabbit, or if fastidious in his appetite, give raw eggs and bread.

If by this little book I have done anything towards interesting those who care about the perpetuation of a wild and interesting animal that is fast disappearing from our hillsides and valleys, and shown that healthy exercise and pleasure can be obtained in protecting him from extinction and by fairly entering the lists against him, I shall have done something towards delaying that sad day when the last badgers, with the lessons of courage and endurance that they can teach, have vanished for ever.

**THE END**

www.ingramcontent.com/pod-product-compliance
Lightning Source LLC
Chambersburg PA
CBHW032015010726
47493CB00007B/2412